The LONELY SCARECROW

by Tim Preston illustrated by Maggie Kneen

FENN PUBLISHING COMPANY LTD.

In the middle of a field,
under a sky the color of cornflowers,
stood a scarecrow.
He had a scary face but a kindly heart.
More than anything, he wished that
the animals and birds
would be his friends.

But the creatures of the field
were afraid of the scarecrow's
flapping coat and big black hat.
They were afraid of his
beady eyes, his crooked nose,
and his jagged metal mouth.

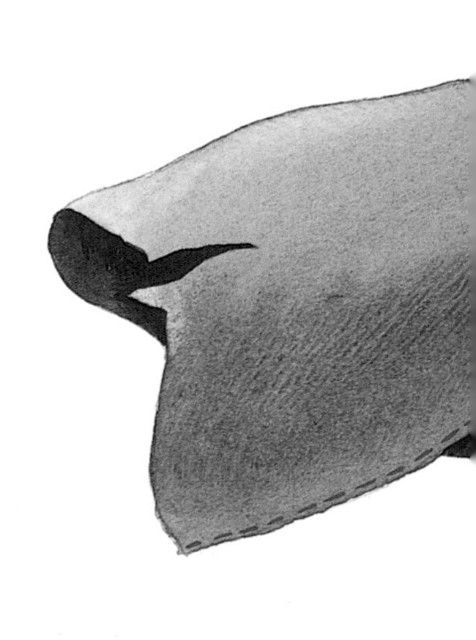

In the spring, the scarecrow watched the animals play at the edge of his field.

He watched the birds as they made their nests.

He watched the carefree tumblings of fox cubs and rabbits.
He listened to the noisy ducklings by the old pond.
And all the time, the animals watched the scary scarecrow.
But they never came near.

Each day, the swaying wheat in the field grew taller.
The scarecrow lost sight of the animals.
He lost even the happy song of the lark,
drowned out by the whispering of the wheat.
Marooned in his golden sea,
the scarecrow lost hope of ever
making friends.

Then the combine monster came
to harvest the wheat.
The animals hid from its churning jaws—
and the ravaged acres of mud and
stubble that it left behind.
They also hid from the
scarecrow, who stood alone
now in the empty field.

From the north came a sly breeze
that stole the leaves from the trees
and the light from the days.
The animals hurried home to their
warm burrows and cozy nests.

And the scarecrow felt even lonelier, for he knew that winter was coming.

Snow fell heavily one night
and kept on falling.
It fell on the bare, still woods
and on the silent fields.
Slowly it covered the ground
where the scarecrow stood.

In the morning, the animals
woke to a world that had changed.
A thick blanket of snow covered
the frozen earth.

The scarecrow
seemed to have vanished, too.
In his place
stood a jolly snowman!

The creatures played happily in the field, rolling and tumbling in the snow around the scarecrow. And the scarecrow? Well, he was as cheerful and bright as the sunny winter day.

Although he was happy,
the scarecrow was afraid
of what would happen
when he lost his snowy coat.

He was afraid that the animals would
shrink from his twisted shape.
Most of all, he was afraid
he would be alone again.
And then the snow began to thaw....

The snow slipped
off the scarecrow's shoulders and dripped
from the brim of his hat.
When the last patches of snow
fell from his face, the animals
looked up in wonder.
Could the friendly snowman be the same
scary creature they had feared for so long?
As the warmth of spring stirred
the brown earth, the scarecrow felt a
bird peck at his hat and a mouse
nestle in the folds of his coat.
And the scarecrow
knew that he would never be lonely again.

To my Friends—M.K.
To Ellie and William—T.P.
For Annie, my best friend ever!—A.J.(JLH)

A Templar Book

First published in Canada in 1999 by Fenn Publishing Company Ltd
34 Nixon Road, Bolton, Ontario, L7E 1W2, Canada.
Visit us on the World Wide Web at www.hbfenn.com

Devised and produced by The Templar Company plc,
Pippbrook Mill, London Road, Dorking, Surrey, RH4 1JE, Great Britain

Designed by Janie Louise Hunt
Edited by A J Wood

Canadian Cataloguing in Publication Data
Preston, Tim
The lonely scarecrow
ISBN 1-55168-211-7
I. Kneen, Maggie. II. Title.

PZ7.P758Lo 1999 j823'.914 C98-932929-1
Printed in Singapore